I0530525

Beneath the Boughs Unseen

By

JEAN ROVER

Beneath the Boughs Unseen

This is a work of fiction. Names, characters, places, and incidents are products of the author's imagination or are used fictitiously and are not to be construed as real. Any resemblance to actual events, locales, organizations, or persons, living or dead, is entirely coincidental.

Copyright © 2015 Jean Rover
Blue Agate Press
Salem, Oregon

All rights reserved. No part of this book may be reproduced in any form or by any means, without permission in writing from the publisher.

ISBN-13:978-0996713009
ISBN-10:099671300X

Cover art: Josh Huhn, DesignPoint, Inc.
Manufactured in the United States of America

For society's invisible people—the homeless, street kids, the working poor, the mentally ill, the disabled, the down-and-out, the hungry, and many, many more—those incarcerated not by bars, but by our unwillingness to see or care.

CONTENTS

We must be willing to let go of the life we planned
so as to have the life that is waiting for us.

—Joseph Campbell

LOST CHRISTMAS

I don't love you anymore. Standing alone in the cemetery on a cold, gray December afternoon, those words kept echoing in my mind, each one striking like a hammer hitting concrete. I didn't think real love ever died.

Visiting the cemetery was the last thing Bill and I did each Christmas Eve. He always placed the swag on our baby's grave. Then we'd head home to sit by the fire and prop our feet up after days of shopping and the traditional round of parties. Bill mixed hot buttered rums, which we savored before opening our gifts. On Christmas Day, we'd drive across town for dinner with Bill's brother and family. After that, we'd take down the tree, carefully pack the ornaments and lights, then hurry off for a luxurious cruise to some sunny Caribbean spot.

Now, it was just me.

I laid the swag with a huge red bow on the grave of my parents and the one decorated with tiny toy soldiers and drums on that of our stillborn baby. The cemetery was deserted, but then it was Christmas Eve. There would be no celebration at my dark house—no tree, no presents, no carols, no buttered rum toasts.

No Bill.

After fifteen years, he wanted a divorce. I was putting away the Thanksgiving groceries when he picked up a can of black olives and nervously tossed it in the air, "Listen," he said, his blue eyes cold, "I don't love you anymore. I … I'm leaving tonight."

Just like that.

"Are you kidding me?" I sputtered. "What am I supposed to tell our guests?" I pointed to the twenty-pound turkey defrosting on the kitchen counter.

"Tell them anything you like." He set the olives down on the counter with a thud. I just stood there with a carton of heavy whipping cream in my hand.

"You can't just leave. Not *now* for heaven's sake—it's the holidays." I was angry and tired, not to mention stunned. "We need to talk, but I still have a pie to make," I said to the back of his curly, dark head. He slammed the door. The car engine revving in the driveway sounded like a small jet taking off.

Varoom. He was gone.

I stared at the closed door until I heard a dripping sound and realized that I had squeezed the carton of cream so hard it burst. The thick cream dripped into my shoe and made a puddle on the floor.

Bill had been distant and moody for some time, but I thought that was because of the problems at his company— new management, followed by staff shifts, increased workloads, and lots of overtime. On top of that, I still grieved for my mother who died in September after a long illness. It so consumed me, I didn't see the breakup of my marriage coming.

"Why," I asked my mother's headstone, "did this happen to me?" I crouched down on the damp grass. "I tried to do everything right. Plan my life. I lost my child and now Bill." I clutched the headstone. "It wasn't supposed to turn out this way." Hot, bitter tears streaked my cheeks. I needed my mother more than ever, and I wanted to hug my baby boy who would have been ten this year. I only held him briefly when he was born, but I always thought I could see Bill in that little pinched face, dark lips, and curly damp hair peeking from the small cap covering his head.

I stood up, but my knees shook and I felt lightheaded. The tombstones seemed to swirl and mix with the dark, brooding sky. Like a trapped animal, I had an intense urge to flee. I darted past lines of headstones to a path, which led to the parking area where I sought refuge in my car. I rolled down the window and took several gasps of cool air before making my way down the steep, winding cemetery road. When I reached the city street, I drove and drove. Finally, I crossed a bridge and the lights of the city glittered in the rearview mirror. Now, I was on the highway heading toward the Oregon coast. I gripped the wheel and, like a robot, kept going until the traffic thinned and totally disappeared.

In the quiet countryside, I passed modest homes with awkward strings of blinking Christmas lights. Every time I saw a tree sparkling in a window, I fought back tears. I imagined wonderful smells coming from kitchens, families sitting down to dinner, and wide-eyed children anxious for morning to come. I thought again about the baby I had lost. My son. Bill wanted to keep trying, but I couldn't go through that again. I wished now we'd given our baby a name. The light from the warm, yellow windows beckoned, but I was a stranger—passing through to somewhere. I pressed my foot on the accelerator trying to speed away from my sad thoughts.

A large, inflated Santa with his hand raised stood in the front yard of the last farmhouse I passed as if he were waving goodbye. The happy homes disappeared, and I was somewhere in the coastal range, surrounded by tall trees and eerie fog. In the rearview mirror, I only saw darkness. The fog thickened, so I switched on my bright lights and even my windshield wipers. Neither helped much, but I didn't care. Alone on the road, I thought of the families in those cozy houses. I had a family once. In the silent darkness, tears came again, and I struggled to concentrate on my driving.

The low, hanging fog made the pavement wet and slick. It occurred to me that I should slow down and head back. Instead, I turned the heater up a notch, determined to keep going, to get away. When I reached a coastal town, any town, I would find a motel and rest there—maybe have some strong, hot tea to take the chill off and just listen to the comforting pounding of the sea.

I felt dizzy again, then realized the car was sliding. I hit the brakes, but the car jerked, skidded onto the shoulder, and bounced down the embankment. The door flew open; I tumbled out, my body slamming against the ground as the car rolled past me and crashed into a tree. For a moment, I lay still. Was I dead? My head hurt and blood dripped down my face. Sharp pains came from my right leg. I felt cold, very cold. Cracking sounds came from the overturned car, but in the darkness, I could not see the damage. I tried to raise myself on my elbows, but my arms shook. My one leg didn't work. The grassy bank was wet and I shivered.

I would die here—alone in the foggy night. The black emptiness engulfed me, except for what seemed like a small light in the distance. They said that happened when you were dying. You passed through a dark tunnel until you got to the light. Go toward that brightness I told myself. Go. Just go. The light seemed to be getting closer when I thought I heard a voice. God must be calling me. Good, I thought. I had a lot I wanted to say to Him.

"Are you all right?" a male voice asked.

I opened my eyes wide and looked into a big flashlight.

"God? Is that you, God?" I asked.

"Huh? What's that?"

"Where am I?"

The figure in the dark didn't answer. When he pulled the blinding light away from my face and flashed it over my body, I could make out a bulky, bearded man looking out from under a baseball cap, his long hair tied back in a ponytail. In the dim light, he looked like a bum. Then, he turned away from me and walked toward my car. He's probably going after my purse. Once he robs me, he'll leave me here to die—or worse. I was easy pickings for him. I closed my eyes and moaned. They flew open again when I felt him touching my leg. He had set the lantern-like light down on the ground, so I could see him crouching over me. My God! He's going to rape me. My heart pounded in my throat. I was defenseless.

His hand had reached my knee. "That hurts!" I cried. "Please don't hurt me."

"Try and move it," he said. When I obliged, he seemed relieved. "You have a bad sprain there." He moved the light closer to my face, and he wiped blood from my forehead with a corner of his shirt.

As he helped me sit up, I could see the spider veins on his nose and gray hair in his beard and at his temples. I groaned; my whole body felt bruised.

"Good, good," he muttered. At least things are movin'. I've gotta camp just back a ways. We need to get you outta here, so we can take a closer look. Hang on." He lifted me and carried me up the embankment. He smelled musty, like a mixture of onions and tobacco. He set me down when we reached the road. I hobbled on one foot, clutching him for support.

"I feel woozy."

"Easy does it." He picked me up again and carried me the rest of the way.

We reached his camp under a small bridge that appeared to cross a dry gulley. He had a fire going there, and he placed me on a worn sleeping bag next to it. I rested my back against a large boulder. The warmth from the fire felt good, but I couldn't stop shivering. He turned away, fished a tin cup from his backpack, and poured a cup of coffee from the blackened aluminum pot he had warming in the embers aside the fire.

"Drink this slowly. It'll take the chill off." He handed it to me.

My first thought was about cleanliness, but the cup warmed my hands and the strong, black coffee smelled good. With each swallow, I could feel the warmth surging through my body. I was grateful for the caffeine. There wasn't much to his camp. He had a hatchet, rain gear, an old transistor radio, some blankets, a large backpack, a small row of canned goods lined up on top of a pile of weathered newspapers, and a roll of toilet paper. I didn't even want to think about where his latrine might be.

His thick hand reached for what looked like a hunting knife. I shuddered. He's going to slit my throat. Instead, he used it to cut up a T-shirt he pulled from his backpack. He dampened a portion with water from a plastic bottle and bathed the wound on my forehead. Every time he came near me, I caught a whiff of his musty body odor.

"Head wounds always bleed a lot, but it's not too bad. More of a scrape, I'd say. You're gonna have a lot of bruisin' there." He used a piece of the T-shirt to make a bandage and then took the red bandana from around his neck and tied it tightly around my forehead.

He picked up the knife again and came toward me. I set down the coffee cup and braced myself.

"What do you think you're doing?" I yelled.

"I'm gonna cut your pant leg a bit, so I can get to that knee—unless you'd rather take them off." His dark, wild eyes looked amused.

He knows I'm afraid of him. I watched helplessly as he slit the right leg of my jeans just past my knee. I noticed he had a rose tattoo on the top of his right hand. "Who are you?" I demanded.

"John," he said. "And who are you?"

"Helen."

"Well Helen, I don't think your leg is broken, but you gotta terrible sprain there."

"How would you know?"

"I was a medic in the army. Viet Nam. You probably don't remember that one."

He was right. I didn't. "That was my father's war," I said. He didn't answer.

"See here, how swollen it is."

I looked at my knee, which was not only puffy and twice its size, but turning an ugly purple. "It hurts, it really hurts. Please don't press on it anymore."

"Tell me about it," he grumbled. "It's startin' to discolor. What we need is ice, but we don't have none. Sooo, we'll do what we can." He took the strips of T-shirt and started wrapping them around my knee. "It's not much, but compression helps, and it will give you some support. He pushed his backpack under my leg and covered me with a heavy blanket. "It helps if you keep it elevated."

I wondered where that blanket had been. Lice could be crawling all over my body. "I … I really need to be going," I said.

"Ha!" He laughed loudly and shook his head. "That car of yers is totaled. You can't walk and, in case you haven't noticed, we don't have limousine service out here. Get real. You won't be goin' no place for a while."

I sunk back against the boulder. "Maybe you could flag down a car—"

"How many cars have ya heard pass over the bridge lately, huh?" He grinned.

He was right. The night was totally still.

"We're off the main road, ya know."

Actually I didn't. I didn't remember turning, but I could hardly see the yellow line through the thick fog.

He opened a can of baked beans and dumped the contents into a cast iron frying pan. In the firelight, his skin looked leathery. He was dressed for the cold weather with a heavy brown jacket over layers of other clothing, jeans, and heavy boots. The ends of his flannel shirt, with my blood on them, hung below the jacket. He wasn't fat or thin; his bulkiness came from the layers of clothing he wore. He stirred the beans in the pan with a big, tarnished spoon until they started to bubble. He dished up a serving in a dented tin bowl and passed it to me along with a spoon and slice of white bread.

"No thank you. I'm really not hungry." My stomach was in knots, and I couldn't help wondering when he last scrubbed that bowl or anything else.

"Suit yourself." He set the food down next to me and poured more coffee. "It's not much, but it's what I got."

I decided it would be okay to eat the bread, since it came from a wrapped loaf. As soon as I took a bite, I couldn't stop, even though it tasted like cardboard. I didn't realize I was famished. Before long, I gobbled the beans and drank more coffee. John just watched me and then passed the loaf of bread; I took another slice and swallowed that, too.

My eyes teared up. "I haven't had anything to eat since this morning," I said, trying to apologize for the way I bolted down his food. John just smiled. He used the empty bean can for his coffee and wrapped a piece of the T-shirt around it to keep the hot can from burning his hand. He ate his portion of beans right out of the frying pan. If I get out of here alive, I thought, I'll probably die from trench mouth or some other dreadful bacterial infection.

"What are you doin' out here on a night like this," he asked between bites, "all *alone?*"

"I ... I was on my way to visit relatives," I lied. "They're probably out looking for me as we speak." I didn't want him to know I was alone in the world and totally vulnerable. "I must have gotten lost."

"You came barrelin' over the bridge like a bat outta hell." He shook his head and laughed. "In fog as thick as soup. When your car left the road, it sounded like a crash of thunder."

"What are *you* doing here?" I asked eager to change the subject.

"I'm heading toward Tillamook. An old army buddy owns a dairy over there. I'm hopin' to stay in his barn for a while ... once the holidays are over. His wife don't like it none, so I can't stay forever; but I'd like ta winter over there, at least during the worst of the weather. Help out with things while I'm there." He looked at me and grinned, "Sleep with the cows." Then he started to chuckle. "When the ol' lady goes into town ta play bingo, I get to use the shower. Yes

9

siree, God bless bingo." He toasted the foggy air with his steaming tin can.

"You're a homeless man?"

He didn't answer, but looked amused as he took his piece of bread, cleaned the rest of the beans from the frying pan, and washed them down with a hearty swig of coffee.

"I've been on the road now for a little over ten years," he finally said.

"But why out here? Wouldn't it be better to stay at a mission or someplace like that where you'd be warm and have some shelter?"

"I used to hang around those places at least long enough to eat Christmas dinner; but when the weather turns cold, those places fill up. It gets crazy. There's lots of stealin' and drinkin'." He shot me a glance. "And more. You haffta watch your back."

"I would think that would be better than living under a bridge—at least the mission is *clean*." As soon as I said it, I realized it was the wrong thing to say. He gave me a hard look.

"Christmas in the city with all those people millin' around buyin' whatever they want—sort of leaves me feelin' empty—'specially when I barely make it by." He stared at my neck. I was wearing the small diamond pendant necklace Bill gave me on our last anniversary. Here it comes. He's probably going to want that.

"Out here, Christmas is just another damned day. A nice, respectable lady like you probably never thought she'd be spending Christmas Eve with a bum."

I looked away. I didn't know what to say. Suddenly he jumped up. My body stiffened in self-defense, but he didn't come toward me. Instead, he stoked the fire and put on more wood. I was grateful for the warmth.

"I borrowed the wood from a church camp up the road." He laughed again. "They won't miss it none, since they're closed for the winter."

I took that to mean he stole it.

"At the shelter, they give each man a gift of socks, candy, razors, and a bandana. I know a guy there, and he slipped me mine early. You got the bandana wrapped around your head, and we're havin' the candy for dessert." He handed me a peppermint disk and eyed my necklace again. "Probably not the kind of treat a nice lady like you is used to." He pulled a cigarette from his coat pocket and lit it by holding it against a twig from the fire. When he diverted his eyes to light the cigarette, I pulled my jacket up around my neck.

"Isn't there anyone … I mean family … that could help?"

"What family I have don't welcome me. Even at Christmas."

"How did you get here? I mean this place is miles from anywhere."

"I walk a lot, hitch rides, jump a railroad car when I can. Sleep in makeshift places beside rivers and roads. Spent a couple nights in a junk yard sleepin' in one of the old cars there."

"But you're able-bodied. I mean you could work. Don't you ever work?"

"Oh, that's a great idea." He slapped his knee and hooted. "And how is some nice boss supposed to get in touch with me? We not only don't have a limousine service out here, we don't have a telephone, neither." He took a long drag from his cigarette and looked out toward the heavy brush surrounding the bridge.

"I just thought if you could it … it would make things easier."

11

"When I was a kid, I did okay in high school and even did a term at the community college, but I flunked out and then got drafted. After the war, I came back to the States but nobody seemed to care. It was like I didn't exist. Finally landed some work on assembly lines and in warehouses. Got married. Did a little weed. Got fired. Had a baby boy. Did some heroine. Got divorced. Then it was on-and-off at gas stations, packing plants, even washed dishes in a hotel. Got fired some more. Well, that's my story."

"I see," I said. I didn't really, but I felt like I had to say something after hearing his life story which was so different from mine and mostly downhill.

"The best job I ever had was workin' in a grocery store, because I could steal the food. Problem was I got into the wine. Then they nabbed me." He paused and looked directly at me. "Ended up in the slammer after that."

I gasped. John was a thief and a substance abuser. Who knows, maybe he wasn't just a homeless man; maybe he did worse things. He could be an escaped convict. A murderer. He had a tattoo didn't he? That would explain what he was doing under a bridge miles from civilization, hiding out in the backcountry. I shuddered, thinking I'd be spending the night here trapped in his web.

"On top of everything else, I have … had a drinkin' problem … which is why I like to get out to the country when the holidays roll around. There's lotsa that stuff around then. Most guys will give you a swig, a smoke, or worse."

"Did you steal this food?" I suddenly blurted.

"Would it not taste as good if I did?"

I lowered my eyes. For heaven's sakes, don't get him riled up. Who knows what's in those cigarettes he's smoking. John kept talking. It probably had been a very long time since anyone listened.

12

"I get by using food stamps, collectin' bottles and cans for the deposit money, and goin' through dumpsters. You'd be surprised at the neat stuff you *good* people throw out."

"Dumpsters! Good God. How can you trust what you find? I mean it's in there with God knows what else." John had that big grin on his face again. I think he enjoyed making me uncomfortable. Maybe it was his last chance to get even with a society he believed dumped on him.

"That's the hell of it." For a brief moment, the wild look in his eyes morphed into a strange sadness. "After all these years, folks still don't know I exist."

"You said you had a son. He must be grown up by now. Couldn't he … help?"

"After the wife walked out, she took the kid. She wouldn't let me see him. I have no idea where he is. Never did." John winced when he talked about his boy, the same way I did when I thought of mine.

"That woman was a piece of work, let me tell ya. This wasn't the way it was supposed to turn out." John tossed his cigarette butt into the fire and then lit up again. "Actually, now I'm old enough to collect Social Security, but it's not much since I didn't work much. But those beans and the bread you ate were honestly arrived by. Out here a man doesn't need much—a little food, a warm fire, a bar of soap."

I was glad he mentioned soap. He put out the cigarette and swiftly picked up his knife. I cringed, but then he started whistling while whittling on a tree limb. I guess he was done talking with me. I sat there staring at the fire wishing I were home in my warm bed and wondering if I'd ever see it again. What a mess I'd made of things.

Suddenly, John stood up and seemed to be listening for something. "Okay," he said. "It's time."

"Time? Time for what?" How stupid I was. He's going to finish me off now and who would ever know. Thoughts about Bill and his new friend raced through my mind. They were probably huddled in front of the fire in some nice living room about now—safe and warm, drinking hot buttered rum, opening presents. I was the last to know about her, but everyone else seemed to know all the details. The most crushing blow came when I heard she was pregnant. Those words echoed in my ears again: *I don't love you anymore.* I couldn't help myself. I felt like something was going to explode inside me.

"How could you!" I cried out and then burst into tears.

"Could I what?" John was on his feet in a flash standing over me. I stared at the lacings on his leather, mud-caked boots. "What's the matter? Huh?"

"He left me after fifteen years ... just like that. Love isn't some switch you turn off. He should be here now protecting me, but he's not. He ... he's there ... with her. If you're going to kill me, just do it. I don't even care anymore. I'd be better off dead."

"Kill you?" He looked hurt; then angry. "If I was gonna kill you, I wouldn't have wasted a can of beans on you for Christ sakes." He threw the knife down and it stuck in the ground, the exposed blade gleaming in the firelight. I wiped my eyes on my sleeve. I couldn't look at him.

"Look, lady."

"Helen," I corrected.

"Helen, then. There's a small church up the road a ways. They should be havin' their services about now. I think I heard the singin'. There will be people there that can help you." He handed me the walking stick he whittled, and he helped me up.

Between leaning on him and using the stick, we made our way up the road through the dense fog. He never said another word to me. Still, I had to wonder if he was telling me the truth. I didn't remember passing a church, but then it was so dark and foggy I wasn't sure. And, didn't he say a while back when I asked about cars, that we were off the main road? I couldn't trust my husband; why should I trust a bum? All he'd have to do is shove me down some gulley and that would be the end of me, but what choice did I have? Then again, if there was a church, maybe there would be cars. If one happened to come by, I'd pull away and flag it down. I was trying to decide what else I could do to save myself when I saw it.

It was a small, yet beautiful, white church with a steeple and real candles shining through the windows. A big, green wreath with a red bow hung on the door. As we got closer, I could hear singing. John helped me up the gray, wooden porch steps. "You go ahead now. Just open the doors and make your way in the best you can. If you feel wobbly, lean on that walkin' stick. Now, go." He gave me a little nudge.

I quickly pulled on the door, and then I turned to thank the man that brought me here, but he was gone. That's strange; how quickly he disappeared. I looked down at my feet and saw my purse. John must have put it there. I felt so ashamed for suspecting him. The small congregation stood in the pews and sang, "It Came Upon the Midnight Clear."

I was so happy to see people, I let go of the door and it slammed hard. The people stopped singing and turned to look at me. The minister, a tall, thin older man in a dark suit, sitting next to the pulpit, got up. He held a Bible in his hand. He stood and stared at me through wire-framed glasses. I must have been a sight leaning on a stick in muddied clothes,

15

a red bandana around my forehead, my face bruised, my pant leg ripped up to my knee exposing strips of John's T-shirt.

"My name is Helen Wilson. I've been in an accident. Please help me." I could feel my mouth move, but I couldn't hear the sound of my words. Their faces seemed to be getting closer, and someone called my name.

"Helen. Helen, do you know where you are?"

"At the church," I said. "Please help me. I need to get back home."

"You're in the recovery room. We're going to take you to your room now, Helen."

I opened my eyes and looked into the well-scrubbed face of a young nurse.

"Where am I?" I asked.

"You're in the hospital, Helen. We're taking you to your room now."

"Hospital? Did they bring me here, those church people?"

"You're a little hazy right now, Helen, but the doctor says you'll be fine. Your hypothermia is under control, and we did a little surgery on your leg. Just relax now until we get you back to your room."

The next time I awoke, Dr. Green hovered over me. He told me I scraped my forehead, had torn ligaments in my knee, and a hairline fracture in the bone. I would be able to go home in a few days, but I would need to rest. Once they removed the cast from my leg, there would be physical therapy. He assured me I would be as good as new.

"How did I get here?" I asked. Did I faint at the church?"

"Your car went off the embankment at the cemetery, Helen. The groundskeeper found you there and called the ambulance. You should always fasten your seat belt."

"But I drove to the coast," I said. "I drove and drove until the accident. John, a homeless man, saved me. He told me about his life. I …"

Dr. Green smiled. "They found you just outside the cemetery. You probably were laying there for some time. Out in the cold like that your body starts to shut down and you hallucinate. Fortunately, the groundskeeper came along. You're a lucky woman, Helen."

"But it was so real."

"You'll be all right," he said. "You just need some rest. In a few days you'll feel as good as new." Before leaving, he wrote out a prescription for painkillers.

I went home and eventually recovered, but my experience seemed so real that I could not accept that it was all a hallucination. I had to search for John. I wanted to find him and thank him for saving my life. He had done a good thing, and I had not trusted him—insulted him even. I needed to know that he was okay, and I sincerely wanted to help. Most of all, I wanted him to know that I noticed him. I really noticed him.

When spring came, I asked my friend, Susan, a co-worker at the bank, to go with me. Together, we drove down the road I thought I had taken that night. I took as many side roads as I could and looked for signs of a camp located under a bridge, but I could not find one. I drove around and looked for the church, but it was nowhere. I talked to local people and gas station attendants, but nobody seemed to know about a bridge, a church, or a summer camp. I placed ads in various coastal newspapers, hoping someone would know John, but I never got a single response.

Back in the city, I went to the mission, the Salvation Army and even contacted outreach groups. I described John the best I could, but no one had heard of a homeless man with a rose tattoo on his right hand. I started volunteering at soup kitchens and food banks hoping he would show up, but he never did. I even headed up a food drive and led an effort to find winter coats and blankets for the homeless. My friends said I was obsessed, and Dr. Green suggested counseling; but the more work I did in those places, the better I felt.

Still I could not erase John from my mind. Finally, I drove out to the cemetery and talked with the groundskeeper to see if he might have resembled John; but when a young, thin man with short blond hair greeted me, I knew it couldn't be him. He took the time to describe how he found me, and I thanked him for his efforts.

***

Susan, a human resources manager, shook her head. She'd been very supportive during my recovery, but now her tone was skeptical. "Helen," she said, her eyes level, "you've got to move on. Maybe this John character was really you speaking to yourself. Maybe the answer to your problems was within you all this time, and that was the way it came to the surface. Who knows what's deep down in our consciousness?"

"Even if it was a hallucination, how could I have created all those details about his life?"

"They didn't find you at some church on the way to the coast out in the middle of nowhere, Helen." Her voice was firm as if she were lecturing some employee in trouble. "They found you at the *cemetery*. Your totaled car was *there*. The ambulance picked you up *there*. Those are the hard facts."

Her sharp tone hurt.

"Look, it was Christmas." She reached over and touched my hand. "Christmas is a magical time. Maybe your guardian angel or spirit guide appeared to you in the form of this man,

18

John. Maybe he took you to another place and time to help you get over a broken marriage."

She patted my hand again and her eyes softened. "Helen, listen to me. You're a smart woman, and you can get that promotion at the bank. In a few years, you'll be making more money than Bill ever did—but you have to put this … this … whatever it is … behind you before it sinks you. You've got your whole life ahead of you."

***

A year had passed and another cold, gray December had come. I was busy preparing for all of the events—not corporate cocktail parties or tinsel-laden celebrations—but fundraisers and food drives. I remembered that Christmas a year ago; how lost I was, and how glad I felt to be alive and well.

I had quit my job at the bank and taken one with a social service agency. At night, I attended college working toward a master's degree in social work. My goal was to work with homeless children. I'd met George there. He was a wonderful, compassionate man who planned to be a high school counselor. I learned to trust again, and we even talked of doing a stint in the Peace Corps together once we graduated. How far my life had come.

I was in the garage loading canned goods into the car to take to the food bank when I spied the pile of muddy clothes I'd worn that night. The hospital had put everything into a plastic bag and handed it to me when I checked out. I never bothered to clean them; I simply threw the bag on top of some other junk in the corner. I decided to toss the clothes into the trash as a symbol of my old self passing away.

I pulled out the muddy sneakers and pitched them one by one into the garbage can with great satisfaction. I reached

19

for the jeans with the cut leg and the rumpled sweater I'd worn and hurled them. It didn't matter if John was real or not—that was the irony of the whole sordid episode. What mattered is that meeting him changed the direction of my life. I pulled out the jacket still caked with mud and happily gave it a final, triumphant shake. Then I saw *it*. The bloodied, red bandana shook loose and lay at my feet.

Hope
Sometimes that's all you have
When you have nothing else.
If you have it, you have everything.
—Anonymous

MILDRED'S SECRET

The gingerbread men lay in a line on the kitchen counter like a class of uniformed schoolchildren ready to march to an assembly. Some had jerky smiles; others looked like they needed eye muscle surgery.

Mildred squeezed strips of white frosting onto the last row. "You know, it's the arthritis in my hands that makes things bumpy," she said to her friend Edna, "but at least they're all smiling."

Edna laughed. "That last one looks a little drunk."

In spite of her arthritis and seventy-some years, Mildred—tall, slim with a full head of silver curly hair—was still an attractive woman. Her lips formed a natural smile, giving her face a pleasant, peaceful look.

She set the final batch of awkwardly decorated gingerbread men on the counter next to a luscious assortment of her other sweet delicacies: peanut butter, chocolate chip, star-shaped sugar cookies, and her specialty—decadent, chocolate-frosted brownies.

The coffee maker gurgled, adding its aroma to the buttery air, making Mildred's small kitchen in the apartment complex for seniors seem cheerful against the grip of another cold December day. Outside, morning frost still clung to the stiff grass, and a cold wind continued to nurture leftover ice around the edges of the windows. Sunshine, Mildred's orange-striped cat, huddled in her bed close to the baseboard heater.

Edna pointed to the counter. "What're you gonna do with all those ... those ... cookies?"

Mildred poured hot coffee into two dark green mugs decorated with rosy-cheeked Santas. "I plan to give them away as gifts. One box is for Nelda. She has no family to speak of, and she hardly gets out anymore. And uh ... I have some friends I plan to call on."

Edna felt a twinge of envy. Judging by the number of cookies on Mildred's counter, she must know tons of people. All of Edna's friends had evaporated. Then, again, maybe they were really Gilbert's friends. After he died, she was all alone. Edna reached for a dark chocolate brownie studded with walnuts. "I shouldn't be eating this. I got a touch of the diabetes, you know."

"A touch?" Mildred wiped her hands on a kitchen towel. She lined up boxes on her counter to package the cookies.

Edna sunk her teeth into the brownie and washed it down with a swig of coffee. Edna was always talking about losing her stomach, but it still bulged there like a tightly inflated beach ball. She was a stocky woman with thinning, mousy gray hair that she parted in the middle and wound into a knot at the base of her skull. Her heavy breasts almost met her stomach under the loose purple dress she wore. "The doc said I need to get rid of my stomach, but I'm gonna wait till after the holidays to work on that."

22

Mildred stopped and filled a green tree-shaped tray with cookies. She stretched clear plastic wrap across the top and handed it to Edna. "Put these in the freezer. When you feel like you need energy, just take *one* and eat it slowly."

A widow, Mildred had moved into Pleasant Point Villa in the fall. Each apartment had one bedroom, a small bath and a combined kitchen, dining and living area. She'd met Edna one sunny September afternoon in the courtyard.

A dyed-in-the-wool fussbudget, Edna didn't make friends easily. She quit going to church after she got into an argument with the new minister because *she* allowed guitar music at the morning service. Hymns, in Edna's opinion, only sounded spiritual when played on an organ or piano, and she thought ministers should be men. Her apartment was either too hot or too cold, the lounge was drafty, and the mail always came too late. When other tenants heard the tap, tap, tap of Edna's black cane, they quickly disappeared like geese escaping winter. Mildred was her only friend.

"I don't bake anymore," Edna said. "My son sends one of the grandkids to pick me up for Christmas. I usually take my special red Jell-O salad that I make with marshmallows and a can of fruit cocktail." Her lips tightened. "They don't even appreciate it. I bring most of it back with me, eat off it for days, and then toss it out. It gets rubbery sitting in the fridge."

Mildred rinsed the bowl she'd used to mix frosting. "You have family, and they probably send you home with a nice gift."

"Oh yeah—bath salts, a can of mixed nuts, maybe a candle … lots of tea. I got tea coming out the wazoo. If I get another kitchen towel, I could make a quilt. You got family close-by?"

"No. My siblings are gone, except for a brother that lives clear over in Vermont and a few scattered nieces and nephews. Ed and I never had children, but being a teacher, I was always around youngsters."

"So what're you gonna do tomorrow? Spend Christmas with your *friends*?" Edna stared at the cookies.

"I'm going to stay right here with Sunshine."

"That's sad that you don't have some place to go ... and lonely."

"No. I get up early, take my walk, weather permitting, make something special for Sunshine, and cook myself a nice meal. Afterward, we just curl up with a good book. People try to lump this wonderful season into one day, when what we really need to do is spread it out over the year. Don't you think?"

"Harrumph," Edna muttered. She'd already had enough of the holiday. The artificial tree in the lounge blocked the sunlight, and she had to dodge that stupid, grinning bell ringer down at the shopping center who was just after her money. She'd had enough of those damn Christmas carols— why did she have to listen to "Jingle Bells" at the grocery store when all she wanted was a carton of cottage cheese?

Sure, she had family, a place to go, but it made her feel like a nut without its bolt. Most of the other guests were from her snooty daughter-in-law's side. The great-grandkids ran around like a bunch of wild hoodlums making more noise than her nerves could handle. Edna just sat in the corner and tried to make conversation with her son's father-in-law who was hard of hearing, blew his nose too often, and told the same corny jokes. Last year he even passed gas. It didn't faze him; he just kept talking. "Did ya hear the one about the two men that got lost when they were out huntin'?" he chortled. A frazzled Edna looked away, but she wanted to yell, "Yeah

at least a hundred times, and did ya think I didn't smell that?"
She was grateful when they drove her home to her cold, dark
apartment carrying the gifts she didn't need and her bowl of
barely eaten Jell-O.

Mildred lined the gift boxes on her counter with
parchment paper and filled each with an assortment of
cookies. All of the boxes were the same size, except for one.

Edna eyed the big box. "That sure is a lot of cookies for
Nelda."

"Oh, this one isn't for Nelda. It's for a special friend."

"Special friend? Someone you've known for a long
time?" Edna studied Mildred's face.

"Not really, but I'm sure he'll enjoy them."

"*He?*" Edna gasped. She sat up like she'd been pricked
with a hat pin.

"Now, where did I put that ribbon?"

"Where did you meet *him?*" Edna leaned forward
anxiously awaiting details.

Mildred counted cookies. "I don't want anybody to get
too much of one thing." She smiled.

Edna winced. She set down her coffee mug. Maybe
Mildred had a secret beau. If that were true, she might move
away, and then she'd lose her one friend. Mildred must've
been quite a looker when she was young. Intelligent, too—
her tiny apartment was crammed with books, and she always
had her nose in one of them. "You better watch yourself in
Nelda's neighborhood. There's lotsa crime in the north part
of town. There's stealing, drugs, and graffiti everywhere."

While Mildred wrapped her packages of cookies in red
paper, Edna continued her tirade. "There's lotsa mixed what-
nots over there and way too many of them Mexicans. Why, I
bet most of 'em came in the back door. All my people went

through the right channels and waited their turn to get into this country."

Mildred carefully topped each wrapped box with an elegant white bow, except for the larger package. That one got a special silver one. "That's just about perfect," she said, admiring the special loops and curls she made with the shiny ribbon. "I didn't think my hands could do that anymore."

Edna stared at the big box and then at Mildred. "You're sure goin' through lots of trouble for your *gentleman* friend."

"Everybody needs to feel special at Christmas." Mildred offered no other information, so Edna started in on Nelda's neighborhood again.

"And those street kids that hang out at that park across from her place. I don't know how Nelda handles it."

"Nicky, one of those boys, helped me that time Nelda tripped on the sidewalk after we'd gone grocery shopping."

"Nicky! You know his name? I'd be mighty careful who you're chattin' up over there. First thing you know, he'll steal your purse."

"When Nelda went down, her bag of groceries spilled all over the sidewalk. Nicky stayed with me until the ambulance arrived. Then he helped pick things up. He even got a broom and swept up the glass from that jar of pickles we lost."

"Mildred, he's a street kid!" Edna squawked. "Hanging around all day, out for no good, and we're all paying for it with our taxes."

"He seemed like a nice young man down on his luck. I gave him a loaf of bread and a package of sliced cheese."

"You're s-o-o-o naïve."

"He looked thin. At first, he was reluctant to take the stuff. Waved me away, like accepting it embarrassed him. When I insisted, he said 'thank you,' and then ran off. There was just something in his eyes ... about the way he looked at me … I can't explain it. I think, maybe, he used to live in that building. He sure knew where to find the broom."

"His eyes! He probably was zonked on drugs. Mildred, he could be a gang member!" Edna's voice went up. "When they're on drugs, they don't care what they do!"

Mildred seemed deep in thought and didn't respond. Instead, she stacked the wrapped cookie boxes in a brown paper shopping bag. Finally, she said, "I think I *get* Nicky."

Edna stood up. "I suppose you better get going if you're gonna get those delivered." She reached for her cane. "I wouldn't want to be in that neighborhood after dark, and it's cold enough to freeze every hair on your head. Maybe you should get that *special* friend of yours to go with you." Edna eyed Mildred, hoping she'd say more about her gentleman, but Mildred just went to the closet and pulled out her coat. She wrapped a red wool scarf around her neck and covered her silver curls with a matching red hat.

***

Edna waited on the sidewalk and watched until Mildred's green Chevrolet disappeared around the corner. A tight, envious twinge crept through her body. She pictured Mildred and her new man-friend laughing over eggnog and having dinner together. Edna slowly tapped her way back to the apartment complex. Maybe this year, she'd bring green Jell-O.

***

Mildred pulled up in front of Nelda's apartment building and luckily found a parking spot on the narrow street. The sky was gray with a few threatening, angry-looking clouds in the distance. The neighborhood seemed unusually quiet, the street deserted, as if all the people had gone inside to avoid the cold. She got out of her car and grabbed a package of cookies for Nelda. A wide smile covered her face as she stepped over bits of paper, an empty beer can, and other trash that littered the street. She rang the apartment building bell, waited, and then headed up the stairs.

She never looked back.

***

Nicky poked his head around a tree in the park. He'd been watching the grandmother lady arrange something in the back seat. When she disappeared into the building, he tossed his cigarette down, mashed it on the sidewalk, and pulled his black wool cap over his ears.

Like a cat closing in on its prey, he quickly crossed the street, peered into the window, and spotted the wrapped packages. He stared at the big box with the fancy silver bow that Mildred had left close to the door. He walked by again, looked over his shoulder, and tried the door handle. It was unlocked! He glanced up and down the street.

It wasn't like he was stealing. No. She'd be giving these things away and to people that had more than he did. In one fast swoop, he snatched up the big package and the shopping bag. He'd done it so many times before in those convenience stores—waited until the lone attendant turned his head, grabbed something, and ran like hell.

He didn't stop running until he was safely in the alley. Gasping, he could see the clouds his breath made in the air. God it was cold. He crouched behind a dumpster that smelled like vomit. Then he reached for that big box. Hopefully, it held something he could trade for a joint. He tore off the beautiful silver bow, ripped the red paper like a little kid on Christmas morning, and pulled the lid off the box.

"Cookies," he muttered. "Shit! Well, what the hell." He couldn't resist. Man he was hungry, and he could feel the December chill deep in his spine. He reached for one of Mildred's silly gingerbread men. "Sorry fellow," he said and

28

bit off its head. Next, he grabbed a peanut butter cookie, then a chocolate chip and swallowed them fast. He fumbled with the shopping bag, found a second box, and tore off the wrapping. "More shit ass cookies!"

He wiped his mouth on his already soiled jacket and devoured a chocolate brownie. A knot welled up inside. In a flash of memory, he suddenly saw his grandmother. She was standing by the door of their apartment handing him a brown bag. "*Escúchame.* Don't lose your lunch. I put in two of my special cinnamon cookies."

"*Mi Abuela,*" he said to the empty, cold alley. She always saw to it that he and his little sister got a Christmas gift, even if it was just a small plastic toy or something she knitted. They couldn't afford a tree, so his Lita would make little decorations and hang them on that discarded palm tree plant she rescued from the hallway. She could nurse anything back to health, except herself. Now, his Lita was gone, and his sister was living with some guy in Albuquerque.

Once his grandmother died, everything fell apart. They got kicked out of their apartment, his mother moved in with one of her endless boyfriends, and Nicky found himself on the street. It seemed like he'd been out there forever, sleeping in a friend's damp basement one night and under a bridge the next. Now, he and two other guys usually bedded down in a decaying building, but they had to wait until it got really dark before they made their way over that chain link fence.

The sweet smell of chocolate and spices kept taking him back to the little dingy apartment—his last secure place. He felt his grandmother's brown hands covering him with a warm quilt and patting his shoulder before turning out the light. Where had all that gone? Tears glistened in his eyes, but it did no good to cry on the street. If guys thought you were weak, they just beat on you … or worse.

"Make me proud," his abuela would say whenever he screwed up. "Make me proud." She even said it that time he "borrowed" a bike and a cop knocked on their door. Only then, his Lita was the one in tears. How the hell was he supposed to do that now? Maybe he should just end it, find a bridge and slither over the side into the Willamette River. If he got high enough on some weed, he probably could do it. If he got his hands on enough crank, he was sure he could. He heard of a guy who killed himself by drinking antifreeze, but that seemed messy.

Make me proud, Nicky. Make me proud. The words seemed to echo in the alley bouncing off the cold brick walls. He shouldn't have stolen the packages from that grandmother lady. The nice lady who always smiled at him, stopped to say hello, and gave him a loaf of bread that time. Other people glanced away when they saw him, as if he was some slimy reptile, but she always looked right into his face, like he was somebody. Hell, he didn't even know her name.

Maybe he could put the packages back. He stared at the torn pieces of red wrapping paper, the muddied silver bow sullied by the damp, dirty alley, the crumbs on his lap. No, he couldn't fix it, and he'd never make anyone proud. His stomach felt sour; he could hardly swallow. He wanted to cry, but the tears wouldn't come. He was alone, and it never was going to change. He needed to do it. Find that bridge. Jump.

A gust of chilly wind blew pieces of wrapping paper down the alley, and the sky started to spit sleet. Nicky pulled the big box to his lap and reached for the lid. *What's this?* In his haste, he hadn't noticed it. Wedged between rows of cookies was a folded note with his name on it. Was this some kind of a dream? Maybe he was freezing to death and his brain went numb. He held it up to the light and squinted.

Sure enough, the note said *Nicky*. He flipped it open. Inside was a message written in the grandmother lady's shaky hand:

I hoped you would take these and open the big box first. Not to worry, I made these cookies especially for you. Please enjoy, and share them with your friends. They are my gift to you. Your gift to me will be to remember this kindness and to never, never give up hope. Merry Christmas—M.

*Looking into the spirit of others is sometimes
like looking into a pond. Though we aim to see
what's deep in the bottom, we are often
distracted by our own reflection.*
—*Katina Ferguson*

THANKSGIVING—*ALONE*

Maggie twisted the ends of her curly brown hair and stared down at the rush-hour traffic from her cubicle on the tenth floor of Comstock Mutual. A long line of red taillights snaked around the block.

The thought of driving home in the heavy Wednesday night traffic, plus the conversation she'd had with her mother over the weekend made her reach into her desk drawer for the Tylenol.

"You can't spend Thanksgiving *alone,*" her mother had wailed into the phone from the East Coast.

"Why not?" Maggie replied. "It's just a day when people overeat, watch football, and get ready for Black Friday. Frankly, the idea of people sitting around a turkey sacrifice isn't particularly appealing to us vegetarians."

"If no one out there in Or-eh-gone invites you, I'll wire you money for an airplane ticket, so you can spend the holiday with your Aunt Bea. I'll call her right now and tell her you're coming."

"No! I ... uh ... I'm planning to be at Carol's again," Maggie lied. Flying to Seattle for a day with stodgy Aunt Bea was the last thing Maggie wanted to do. Oh, her Aunt was okay, but she was a compulsive knitter. The clack, clack of knitting needles started at breakfast and didn't stop until Aunt Bea dozed off during the Bill O'Reilly show, head back, mouth open, snoring like a pig in distress. The last time Maggie visited, she left with an ugly beanie hat she'd never wear, a "cute" dishcloth, and Aunt Bea's pride and joy, a knitted garden slug complete with huge eyes and a red wool Angelina Jolie mouth.

Maggie's vegetarian lifestyle also baffled her mom. "Make sure you get enough protein. I don't think you're getting enough protein." And finally, "What did I ever do to make you so ... so eccentric? Most women your age have prospects. Have you met anyone—?"

Maggie popped the Tylenol capsule into her mouth, tipped her expensive persimmon-tinted water bottle, and swallowed. Ever since she took a job in Portland three years ago, her mother obsessed about her being alone on Thanksgiving. So did everyone else for that matter.

"You're welcome to join us again," Carol, her co-worker, had said. Carol's family always ate in a hurry, so she could go on her driving marathon—dropping the kids off for dinner with her ex, and then racing across town to join her second husband's folks. Last year, Maggie had contributed a pumpkin pie, but ended up taking it home because there wasn't time for dessert.

"Why don't you come over and hang with us," Sylvia, her gym partner suggested. "It's just going to be Ron and me, my kids, his kids, the in-laws, my divorced grandmother, and her ... uh ... quirky boyfriend. We're having pizza this year. You can pick off the pepperoni."

33

"Thanks for thinking of me," Maggie had told all of them, "But I have plans." Actually, she was just going to relax at home. *Alone*. While she appreciated the invitations, she hated the frenzy, and she found it impossible to meld with other people's families. She spent most of the time checking her watch and feeling like a stray. For some reason, she always drew the seat next to the difficult geezers. "You can get a really good buy on bananas at WinCo," said somebody's Uncle Gilbert, while adjusting his hearing aid. He then spent the next half-hour explaining the ins-and-outs of garage door openers in an overly loud voice. Across the table was the dyed-in-the-wool partisan geezer. "We wouldn't be having these problems now if, back then, Clinton had kept his pants zipped. Cut taxes …cut taxes … cut taxes."

Then there were *those questions*: "You're not having turkey? Is it some sort of a religious thing?" Followed by *those observations*: "It's not Thanksgiving without turkey. We heard you were a picky eater."

After she passed up Aunt Freda's special Mandarin orange Jell-O salad with sliced bananas, they said, "There's no meat in there, honey." Maggie didn't think it was polite to point out that gelatin was made from boiling animal tendons and bones, so she just smiled. Aunt Freda glared.

The family insider stuff was more frustrating. "Emma just can't stand being alone since Fred died. He isn't even cold, and already she's in bed with some guy she met down at the senior center." Who was Emma?

"I told Blair she could bring her boyfriend, but they'd have to sleep in separate rooms. Pass the yams." Blair must be the young brunette at the far end with the nose ring and pout.

"I'm getting up at 4 a.m. tomorrow, so I can get to the sock sale," said a plumpish woman with thinning helmet hair.

"They're fifty percent off!" She popped an olive into her mouth. "They're givin' away free coffee and doughnuts, too. Well, you can't have too many socks."

After dinner, the men disappeared to watch football and drink beer—never to be heard from again, except for those wild whoops when their favorite team scored.

So much for Thanksgiving.

That Norman Rockwell painting of the large extended family sitting around the table with big smiles on their faces wasn't reality. Today's families were cut-and-paste, constantly checking cell phones, fiddling with tablets, and always on edge. Thanksgiving was a blip on the horizon—a brief November moment between Halloween and the big Christmas shopping rush.

Why can't people get used to the idea that being alone doesn't mean you're lonely? Maggie tossed a credit report in her out basket. *I'm just going to curl up with the cat and a good book. I'll have a veggie burger, maybe plug in the bread machine. Besides, Thanksgiving is about gratitude, not feasting.*

"Earth to Maggie," said the voice above her. She looked up from her desk. There rubbing his back like a cow against the entrance panel of her cubicle, was tall, nerdy Steven from accounting. He peered at her through wire-framed glasses and wore that tweed suit that never seemed quite right on his lanky body.

That's soooo Steven. "Gee, I'd offer you a salt lick, if I had one," she said sarcastically, giving him the coldest stare her green eyes could muster.

Steven winced. "Sorry, I'm an outdoor guy. This suit is scratchy. But hey, if you're not doing anything around noon tomorrow, we could use some help serving down at the mission. We're expecting a big crowd."

She smiled at him. "Thanks, I've got *plans*."

He loosened his tie and stretched his neck. "There's lotsa hungry folks these days."

"Yeah right. They bring those homeless guys in off the street. Then after feeding them *one* meal, they send them back out into the cold—still homeless. Go figure." Her computer dinged, indicating she had e-mail.

He folded his arms and straightened his body. "Hope," he said and paused, "*begins* with a good meal. I would think *you* with all your talk about compassion for all beings would get *that*."

"Uh-huh," she said, half-listening, reading her e-mail, which was from her supervisor. He wished everyone a happy turkey day. "Sheesh!"

"If you change your mind, let me know. We're kinda shorthanded this year."

"Like I said, I've got plans." Steven never gave up. He always stopped by to chat or to drop an invitation. "Wanna go on a bike ride? How about a hike? I've got tickets to the Trail Blazers game." He couldn't get it through his bean-counting head that he just wasn't Maggie's type. She was Nordstrom; he was Sears … and a … a … dork. She watched him move on to the next cubicle, exhaled a long, deep breath, and reached for the last item in her in-basket. "Someday my prince will come," she muttered to herself.

***

On Thursday morning Maggie—no makeup, dressed in sweats and sneakers, thick brown hair in a careless ponytail—settled down on the couch with the extra-fat newspaper. The smell of bread baking in her trendy bread machine wafted from the kitchen. A Mozart sonata played on the stereo. Maggie pulled out the thick wad of advertising flyers from the newspaper. She shook her head and tossed them on the floor.

She laughed watching Vera, her calico cat, bat and attack Grog, her name for Aunt Bea's knitted slug. "Aw geez," she groaned when the phone rang, bracing herself for her mother's shrill voice.

Instead, it was Vi, her neighbor across the street. "I noticed your car was in the driveway. I thought that maybe you were spending Thanksgiving *alone*. Why don't you join us? Curt will be here."

"Thank you, but I'm ... uh, I'm going out later." My God, why did she say that? The woman had a direct view of her house, and nosey Vi was one of those people who knew everything that went on in the neighborhood. If Maggie stayed home, Vi would know it, consider it a snub, and never let her forget it. Maggie depended on her to take care of her house and Vera when she was out of town. Getting the cold shoulder from Vi was like being marooned on a chunk of drifting sea ice with a hungry polar bear.

And Curt. God. That's really why Vi extended the invitation. She'd been trying for months to match her up with her tubby, twice-divorced brother-in-law, who talked endlessly about his gun collection and bowling. His idea of a night on the town was a trip to Burger King for a Triple Whopper.

Where could she hide out? Shopping? Most of the stores were closed. The library? The gym? They'd be closed too. A movie? Hmmmm.

"You're joining friends then? Anybody I know? A guy?"

"Actually, I ... uh ... I'm going downtown to help serve the homeless." It seemed like a Vi-proof answer. "And, uh ... we're all getting together afterwards ... you know, for a party of sorts."

"How nice," Vi cooed. In an instant, she hung up.

***

37

"How do I get myself into these things," Maggie grumbled as she parked her car on the street and walked the few blocks to the mission. It was chilly outside and, except for Christmas decorations everywhere, the deserted city seemed like an empty, concrete tomb.

"I'm so glad you showed," a delighted Steven said. "One of our servers called in sick." He was wearing a red slipover sweater that clashed with his reddish brown hair; the blue denim shirt peeking through the top desperately needed to meet an iron.

That's soooo Steven.

She tied on a white apron and went to work scooping up mashed potatoes. Next to her stood Mel, an older man with glasses, bald head, and a bulging stomach under his apron. Mel was in charge of dressing and green beans.

Soon the down-and-outers filed in—men with leathery faces and haunted, faraway looks, and women with stringy hair and missing teeth. Some wore clothes they'd obviously slept in. A man with a scarred face carried on a loud conversation with Jesus. Two others were in wheelchairs; one had no legs, just stumps jutting from the seat. "God bless you," he said repeatedly. The musty odor mingling with the homey aroma of turkey and coffee smelled like something gone bad in the fridge.

Then the families started to come—embarrassed fathers and anxious looking mothers shepherding big-eyed kids. There were groups of street kids in hoodies and baggy pants, carrying their belongings in backpacks, and men in worn, crumpled army fatigues.

Maggie had never seen so many hungry, homeless people. She dished up generous helpings of mashed potatoes and slathered on the gravy, even though she didn't approve of it.

"Be careful what you're doing there." Mel banged his serving spoon against the metal bin. "You gotta watch yer portions, or we're gonna run out." His criticism stung. Maggie tried to think of a sharp response, when she heard a small voice.

"I don't like gravy." A little blond girl looked up at her.

"How about butter? Do you like butter?"

"I want ice cream." She squirmed in her ill-fitting, blue cotton dress. Her worn red jacket had stains around the cuffs.

Maggie stared at the child. The curly blond hair, blue eyes, and dress on that small body seemed familiar. She was almost the picture of the doll Maggie yearned for in the window of the variety store when she was a child. Her father surprised her with it for Christmas and which, although worn, was still somewhere in the attic back home. It probably was the only time in her life she'd gotten exactly what she wished for. She remembered it forever. "We don't have ice cream, sweetie."

"We get to have pumpkin pie, kiddo," her mother quickly added, trying to distract her daughter. She was a young woman whose own dark blond hair was pulled back into a ponytail. She wore no makeup. Her blue eyes looked tired. Maggie wasn't sure, but thought she might be pregnant.

The little girl's mouth tightened. "I want ice cream," she insisted, her eyes pleading.

"Do you want dressing?" Mel barked at the mother.

Startled, she nodded, and then shepherded her daughter down the line. Maggie watched as the woman put slices of pie on her tray. They walked over to one of the long tables and sat down among what seemed like rows of gray men. The mother took the rolls off their plates, wrapped them in a paper napkin, and slipped the bundle into her coat pocket.

"Do we happen to have any ice cream back there?" Maggie asked Mel.

"Look, if we haffta stop and fill individual requests, we'll be here for the next two months," he grumbled. "They get pie and they're lucky to get that."

Maggie's face flushed. What an insensitive grump. A limp brown curl hung loose at her ear. Someone from the kitchen brought out a fresh bin of mashed potatoes.

Just then, Steven appeared at her arm. "Don't mind Mel," he whispered. "His wife makes him do this every year." He shoved a Styrofoam cup with a lid in front of her face and carefully opened it. Inside was a healthy scoop of vanilla ice cream. He winked. "I know where they keep their stash."

He walked over to the table where the little girl sat and handed her the cup and a plastic spoon. He brought his finger to his lips and made a *shhhhhh* sound. The little girl squealed and clapped her hands. Her mother glanced at Maggie and smiled. Maggie grinned sheepishly. She'd let the request drop. Steven was the one who made the ice cream magically appear.

At last, the serving line thinned to a trickle. It was time to think about cleaning up. There were trash barrels filled with paper plates, cups, and crumpled napkins. A floor crew busied itself stacking trays and wiping tables. The little blond girl and her mother had lingered in the warmth as long as they could. Now, Maggie watched them go out into the cold. *Where would they sleep tonight? On the streets? In a car?*

"We had a good turnout. Thanks for coming," Steven stood beside her again.

"That was nice, what you did with the ice cream," Maggie said.

"I made one kid's wish come true, but I can't help wondering how many other ones wanted ice cream, too."

Maggie swallowed hard. How true that was. Hunger wasn't just over *there* in third-world countries. It was *here* in her backyard. Homeless people weren't just bums and panhandlers or those with mental or substance abuse problems, but everyday folks who were down on their luck. Good people that woke up one day and found their jobs gone, bills looming, rent skyrocketing, and their lives turned upside down. How could she have missed that? She tried hard to live a lifestyle that conserved the earth's finite resources and avoided cruelty, but she'd never really had such a close-up look at hunger. How many more were teetering out there? Her mouth felt dry. She needed water.

"Are you okay?" Steven asked.

"Oh ... me ... yeah." She rubbed her forehead. "I need to find some water."

"Just a minute." He rushed to the kitchen, returned with a glass, handed it to her, and watched as she sipped. Finally, he said, "Listen, if you're not doing anything around the second week in December, we have a lot of fun wrapping toys and packing food boxes for needy families." He took off his glasses, blew on them, and used his sweater to wipe them clean. One of the nose pads was missing.

Maggie stared. *God, that's soooo Stev—* She stopped.

"Are you sure you're okay?" He put his arm around her. "Our real joy is going to their homes and watching their faces when we hand out the stuff."

For the first time Maggie noticed Steven's eyes. They were not just gray but sensitive. Compassionate, even. She studied his face. It no longer seemed nerdy. No, it was ruggedly handsome ... and caring. She reached over and gently patted his arm. "Sure, Steven," she said. "Sure, I definitely want to be there."

To the world, you might just be one person
But to one person, you just might be the world.
—Dr. Seuss

THE PROMISE

Killing your ex-husband isn't what most people think about during the holiday season, but that's exactly what Michelle wanted to do. She hopped from one foot to another trying to stay warm as she stood in line in front of the Save-Mart at 5 a.m. on the Friday after Thanksgiving. There wasn't a drop of moisture in the air, just frost on the rooftops and a chilling wind that invaded her jacket and red wool hat. The biting cold whitened her breath. No wonder they called it Black Friday.

"Damn that Jerry," she muttered. She pictured herself dropping him into an icy green sea from a helicopter. He had promised their two small boys that Santa would bring them the very popular Rambo Danbo game if they were good— his way of keeping them quiet, so he could watch a football game. Now they, like every other kid, had their hearts set on this hot, pricey electronic game.

The Save-Mart line quickly grew until it curled around the corner of the store and spread into the dimly lit parking lot crammed with cars even at this hour. Michelle had never expected anything like this. Several people had camped for hours in the darkness in front of the store entrance. They brought blankets and folding chairs and ate breakfast from Styrofoam containers.

A chubby, middle-aged man stood directly behind her. His big stomach pressed against her as he craned his neck to see if the door was about to open. Michelle spun around and glared at him. He wore a black wool hat, gray jacket, and had a large turned-up nose that seemed out of place on his face. His dull gray eyes avoided her stare. He sipped coffee from a paper Starbucks cup and munched on pastries from a white paper bag. Michelle had skipped breakfast. The coffee sent a twirl of steam into the dark air. The aroma of good coffee coupled with the sweet smell of sugar and fat made her mouth water. Money was so scarce, she couldn't remember the last time she'd had a really good cup of rich, black coffee.

Her thoughts drifted back to Jerry, probably still snoozing in his warm bed, and then to the last conversation she'd had with him—if that's what you could call it. Talking to Jerry was like trying to teach music to a tone-deaf student.

He'd come to her apartment to return the boys after having them for the weekend. Once the kids were out of earshot, Michelle lit into him. "What were you thinking?" she had demanded, her hands on her hips. "All the boys talk about is that silly game."

Jerry hooked his thumbs in the waist of his jeans. He hung his head like a little child in trouble. He needed a shave, and his unkempt brown hair hung over bloodshot eyes. He was in between jobs—again. His gambling habit and allergy to steady work had destroyed their marriage. Despite his dark, once handsome looks, Jerry was about as solid as ice cream on a hot day.

"I can't afford to buy them one," Michelle shouted. "Can you?"

"They'll get over it," he muttered.

"You just don't get it, do you?"

"Get off my back."

"They're children!" She tugged on the thin silver chain around her neck.

"Something will come up," he insisted.

"They *believed* you." The silver chain snapped.

"Maybe I'll get lucky." They left it there. It was always where they left it.

After Jerry stormed out the door, Michelle pulled her shoulder-length, golden brown hair into a ponytail and proceeded to paint her toenails bright red. The vivid color and slow, meticulous brushstrokes had a soothing, meditative effect. By the time she reached the tenth toe with a second coat, the queasy feeling in her stomach had lessened.

The boys, five-year-old Jared and three-year-old Brandon, tried hard to hold up their side of the bargain. When Brandon spilled his cereal, Jared ran for a sponge and wiped up the milk, something he'd never done before the promise of the Rambo Danbo.

"I help," little Brandon said, not wanting Jared to win more favor with Santa.

Jared carried his dinner plate to the sink and picked up all his toys before he went to bed. Brandon did his own awkward imitation but couldn't quite reach the kitchen counter. He cried all the way home from the babysitter's house, because he lost his mittens and thought Santa would hold it against him.

Since the divorce, Michelle worked as a waitress at a nearby sandwich shop. She barely made enough to pay the rent and buy food. Jerry seldom came through with child support.

Everyone at the restaurant liked Michelle. Despite the challenges in her life, she had a friendly disposition and was

on a first-name basis with her regular customers. In between
tuna melts, hamburgers and keeping coffee cups full, she
listened to their chatter and happily exchanged stories about
children. She was twenty-four years old, pretty in a
wholesome way, and it paid off in tips. No one would have
guessed that behind the natural smile and brown attentive
eyes was a life teetering close to the edge.

The unusually cold winter had caused heating costs to
skyrocket. On really frigid days, she and the boys wore jackets
in their small apartment which was located in the basement of
an older, drafty house. However, when little Brandon came
down with a cold and then bronchitis, Michelle turned up the
thermostat. At night, she tucked him into her bed to keep
him warm.

She had hoped to complete a secretarial course so she
could get a better job but dropped out to pay the doctor and
heating bills; then the brakes went out on her second-hand
Dodge Neon. Fortunately, Alma, an older woman who lived
above her, hired her to make slipcovers for her threadbare
love seat. That sewing project and the more generous holiday
tips enabled Michelle to scrape together an extra fifty-five
dollars.

When Michelle heard the Save-Mart was having a "door-
busting" sale on the Rambo Danbo games for forty-eight
dollars instead of the normal eighty-nine, she dragged herself
out of bed at 4:00 a.m. All the trips to Goodwill for clothes,
saying no to movies, candy, toys, and just about everything
else that cost money made her determined to make her
children's wish come true. Sure, it was just a game, but a
promise was a promise—and granting it was within her reach.

"They're opening the doors!" someone near the front of the
line shouted. "Go, go, go!"

45

The crowd surged forward; strange elbows shoved Michelle aside. She tried to push back, but her small stature was no match for the out-of-control wave of people that moved backward and forward until it finally pushed her through the door.

A crowd swarmed around the large table holding boxes of Rambo Danbo games. Michelle managed to squeeze in, but couldn't get to the front until a surge of people behind her thrust her forward. She leaned against a heavy-set woman in a bright blue wool coat to keep from falling. Her awkward tilt created a gap through which she managed to stick her arm and grab one of the games. She was trying to pull it past the woman when another hand suddenly locked onto the box.

"It's mine!" Michelle yelled into the blue coat. She tightened her grasp only to hear the cardboard tear as someone jerked the game away.

"That was *mine*," she wailed to the small piece of packaging she held in her hand.

The woman in the blue coat gave her a dirty look. "Quit leaning on me," she growled.

The public address system crackled, and a male voice announced that the Rambo Danbo game had sold out. The crowd groaned. Then the microphone hissed and popped; strains of "Frosty the Snowman" floated over the din.

"Hurry!" someone shouted. "They've got some screamin' deals on aisle three."

Michelle's heart jumped in her throat, her head ached, and she felt dizzy from skipping breakfast. She needed to get outside in the fresh air, away from the craziness. She hurried past the displays of ornaments, artificial trees, and banks of candy canes. A mechanical Santa waved his arm. "Ho, Ho, Ho, Merry Christmas, Merry Christmas," said his battery-powered voice.

A tall woman, owl-eyed behind thick eyeglasses, hit Michelle with her shopping cart. "Mildred needs a new crock pot," she said to her companion. She didn't even apologize.

In the distance, Michelle saw two young women playing tug-of-war over a red jacket. A store employee wearing reindeer antlers tried to intercede, but ended up on the floor. Michelle fled toward the checkout counters.

Suddenly, she stopped.

The middle-aged man who'd been behind her in line now stood there with an armload of Rambo Danbo games resting on his big stomach. "One for the grandkid," he announced to the people around him. "I'm gonna sell the rest on eBay."

He recognized Michelle from the line. "Say, don't leave empty-handed. I'll sell you one right now for just sixty-five smackers." His pink, fleshy face beamed.

Michelle smirked. One of the games he held had a tear in the packaging. The anonymous hands now belonged to a face and its body to the sleazy underbelly of the secondary market. She felt like she just turned over a rock and was staring at a swarm of creepy dark things moving toward her. She sneered. "I'd rather pay full price than line your pocket."

He shook his head and laughed. "I'm giving you a bargain."

"It's Christmas," she said.

He snickered. His nostrils widened. "That's the point."

"I was ahead of you in line," she shot back. He just turned away leaving her to look at the fat folds at the base of his head.

***

Outside in the parking lot, Michelle welcomed the blast of cold air against her face. Finally, she could breathe. Her hands shook as she turned the ignition key. The engine made a groaning sound but eventually kicked in. "Phew," she sighed. She gunned it and peeled out of the lot making her tires squeal. She didn't stop until she reached an intersection and waited for a red light to change.

Christmas isn't just about presents, but how can I make the kids understand that, especially when their friends get piles of toys and that idiot, Jerry, makes a promise he doesn't plan to keep. Aren't children entitled to some magic in life?

The light turned green. Michelle made her left turn onto a thoroughfare that was busy even at this early hour. She longed to paint her toenails.

Out of nowhere, a police officer wearing a white helmet stepped from the curb and with sharp jabs of his arm motioned for her to turn right. At first, Michelle thought he was redirecting traffic, but then she saw the red and orange "B-B-Q—All You Can Eat" sign and realized she was in an empty restaurant parking lot. She could see the cop's motorcycle cleverly hidden behind a large bush.

Michelle rolled down the window. She took a long swallow.

"Ma'am, I need to see your license, registration, and proof of insurance."

"What's the trouble, officer?"

"Your license, registration, and proof of insurance, please."

Michelle fished the license and insurance card from her purse and pulled the registration from the glove compartment.

"What's the problem?" she asked again.

"The reason I pulled you over," the young officer said, "is because you made an improper left turn."

"I don't understand."

"When you made your left turn, you pulled into the right

lane. You should always pull into the left lane at an intersection. Did you know that?"

"This intersection is controlled by traffic lights, and I have to make a right turn up there." She pointed to the next corner. "I ... I wanted to get over while I could."

"There was plenty of time for you to change lanes, once you made your turn, ma'am." He seemed to be smirking like a hunter that just snared a rabbit. "You know if an oncoming car was making a right turn—"

"Nothing was coming," Michelle interrupted. "If there was, I would not have turned."

"Sometimes there are pedestrians."

"There was nothing ... nothing there," Michelle said firmly.

"It's still dark out, ma'am."

"Nothing!" Her hand slapped the steering wheel. "Absolutely nothing."

"Some people, you know, don't heed stop signs when there's no traffic around, but the law requires that they do so." He sounded like he was talking to a backward child.

"I would never do that."

"I'm not saying that you would." He went off to his motorcycle to check her record.

Michelle waited. *That little snip. His wimpy build makes him look about twelve, and in that white helmet, he looks like a Martian.* She fought off an urge to drive away.

The officer returned, stood in front of her open window, and scribbled something on his pad.

"Are you writing me a ticket?" She leaned her head toward the window, trying to see.

"Yes ma'am." He tore it from the pad and thrust it toward her.

She gasped. "Two hundred and forty-two dollars! For a

minor offense, are you kidding me?"

"You have the right to appeal." There was that smirk again.

"You think this is funny?"

"Ma'am—let's not make things worse." He sounded irritated.

Michelle didn't care. "Worse! How could things get any worse? You just took my Christmas … my savings … the kids won't have anything now …"

"You can explain all that to the judge." He seemed pleased with himself.

"By then, Christmas will be over."

"You need to move on, ma'am." He jutted his chin.

"Children don't understand that they're poor!" she blurted.

"Our conversation is over, ma'am. You have the right to appeal." He sounded like a recording.

"But …"

"Drive safely, ma'am." He turned and walked away.

Michelle started the ignition. Her foot trembled as she pressed the gas pedal. Her head throbbed and she felt cold. Really cold.

After turning right, she pulled into the empty parking lot of a bank. The dizzy feeling returned, and she was afraid to drive farther. She stared at the idyllic snow scene painted on the bank's windows. A string of jolly snowmen in red and green wool hats, peppermint striped scarves, and mittens danced and skied against a background of falling snowflakes. There was no joy in her heart.

She dumped the contents of her purse on the passenger seat. Like an addict seeking a fix, she grabbed her pillbox, popped off the lid, and washed down two ibuprofen tablets with the plastic water bottle she kept in the car. She rubbed her sore neck waiting for the painkillers to take effect. If Jerry hadn't made that reckless promise, she would not have gone to the store and none of this would've happened.

She should not have married Jerry, but in the heat of one passionate moment, just that one moment, she got pregnant. She was only nineteen when Jared was born, and it changed everything. *Everything.* Two years later, she had Brandon. Why did it always take two kids and a few years before a couple realized their life together was a mistake?

The snowmen's smiles seemed to mock her. Their frosty faces and coal black eyes mirrored that big man at Save-Mart laughing because he had a pile of those games; Jerry standing there with that idiotic, ever-present blank look; the woman who bumped her in search of a crock-pot, and that stupid, smirking cop, a real life Grinch. "People are no damn good," she cried. She crumpled over the steering wheel, glad she was alone. At first, the tears slid silently down her face, and then gave way to body shaking sobs. "They're just no damn good."

***

Michelle rose early on Christmas Day. At seven in the morning, the apartment was quiet and icy cold. There was not a sound of traffic on the street. Occasionally, the older gas furnace would kick on and grumble in the background. Every time it did, she hung her feet over the register in the floor and waited for warm air to dry the cherry red polish on her toenails. When her toes were smudge proof, she hid them in a pair of heavy, warm socks. Then she scooped coffee from a can into her coffee maker. While it gurgled and sputtered, she placed three bowls on the table. Even the bowls were cold. She pulled the big yellow Cheerios box from the cupboard and set it next to the jar of peanut butter. The boys would come bounding out any moment anxious to get at their gifts. She'd make their toast after they settled down.

51

Christmas trees were expensive, so she'd covered a small end table with a green towel and decorated her potted philodendron with tiny dime-store ornaments. She taped the awkward glitter-covered star Brandon had made from yellow construction paper to a drinking straw and stuck it in the middle of the pot. Between the plant's flowing vines, she placed a small red candle.

The boys had pinned their stockings to the arm of a living room chair, and Michelle filled them with some candy she got at the mission. She had picked up a small, red plastic fire engine for Jared from the mission's donation center and a blue plastic airplane for Brandon. The mission also gave her socks and underwear. She placed the gifts on the floor next to the end table and decorated plant.

Sipping her bland coffee, she lit the candle and then stood back and sized up the plant and the gifts. At least it looked festive. It wasn't exactly what she'd planned, but it was enough. The boys had gifts, they were all in good health, they had a roof over their heads, and they had each other.

She set a box of mac and cheese next to the stove. They would have that, hot dogs and left over apple pie from the restaurant for lunch. She also took home the split pea soup that wasn't selling well. The soup and some crackers and cheese would be their Christmas dinner.

Suddenly, Jared darted past her in the direction of the philodendron. Brandon was close behind. Michelle made them put on sweaters before they emptied the stockings and tore the paper from the gifts. Then in an act of defiance, she turned up the thermostat. They could at least be warm for one hour on Christmas morning.

"He didn't bring it," Jared shouted when he discovered the red truck. "We asked for a Rambo Danbo, and he didn't bring it." His lower lip trembled.

"Honey, we need to be grateful for what we have." Michelle set down her coffee cup. "Let's take a look at that nice truck."

"I was good, and he didn't bring it." He glared at Brandon as if he had done something to cause this misfortune.

"I good too," Brandon said.

"Maybe he missed our house." Jared pushed a kitchen chair close to the basement window and peered out. "Maybe, if we had a *real* tree." He jumped down, ran back to the decorated plant, and slapped a leaf causing a tiny ornament to fly across the room. "Maybe he didn't know we were here." He clenched his small fists.

Brandon set down his airplane. His brown eyes were big and sad. The Tootsie Roll he chewed left brown slobber on his chin.

"Maybe Santa ran out," Michelle said. "That could happen. Maybe next year—"

"But I told all the kids we were getting one." Jared stamped his little foot. His lower lip jutted into a pout.

"Just look at this neat truck." Michelle tried to distract him. "It even has a ladder that goes up and down."

Jared threw the truck down. "I don't want it! I'm telling Dad!" he wailed. Then he ran off to his bedroom and slammed the door.

Brandon climbed into Michelle's lap and buried his head in her chest. He always got upset when his big brother did. Michelle held him tight and kissed his hair. She wanted to scream. *Go ahead and tell your Dad. That'll do a lot of good. That bastard caused this problem. He ruined our Christmas, not to mention that piggish man at the store and that damn sniveling little cop.*

"Mommy, is Santa mad?" Brandon asked.

"No honey. It's not your fault." She squeezed his

shoulder and rubbed his back.

"Are you going to paint your toenails now?" he wondered. Michelle flinched—not because he asked, but because her little boy had noticed. That was the final straw.

"Mommy, why are you crying?" Brandon asked.

"Oh, honey ... I ..." Before she could finish the doorbell rang—four rapid rings in succession. That had to be Jerry. That was the way he always announced his arrival. Impatient. Self-centered. Annoyed because he had to wait. He hardly gave a person a chance to respond before the sequence of four rings began again.

What was he doing here now? He usually didn't get up until noon. This time she was absolutely going to kill him. Maybe tell him to get the hell out. No, she had a better fate for him. She would make him go and explain to Jared why Santa didn't bring the game. That way he could see close up what a broken promise looked like. She set Brandon down, wiped her eyes on her sleeve and flung open the door ready to do battle.

"Santa!" Brandon shrieked. "Jared! Jared! Hurry! Santa is here! He found us!" He jumped up and down.

Michelle stared. Sure enough, Santa stood there with a young woman wearing a green fur trimmed elf hat that set off her short reddish hair and blue eyes. Michelle didn't recognize the woman, but the man in the padded red suit and white beard seemed familiar. There was something about his gray eyes. They definitely didn't belong to Jerry. Jerry's eyes were dark brown. Maybe this couple had come into the restaurant.

In a flash, Jared came running from his room. He grabbed the gaily-wrapped package from Santa's hands, and he and Brandon ripped the paper away.

"It's a Rambo Danbo!" Jared screamed. "He came. He came. I told you he would!" he said to Brandon, redeeming himself as the big brother. "Thank you! Thank you, Santa!"

Little Brandon ran to Santa. He hugged his knee and darted back to his big brother, leaving a sticky chocolate smear on Santa's leg.

Michelle was speechless, but glad the kids remembered their manners. "How did you know … I mean what they wanted?"

"I'm Santa. I keep lists." She'd heard that voice before.

"I know I should know you, but …"

"Something for you too," the elf interrupted. She handed Michelle a tiny, thin package wrapped in a red bow.

"Thank you." Michelle pressed it against her breast. "Are you folks from the mission?"

"Let's just say we're on one." Santa winked. "This is my big day, you know."

Michelle couldn't resist. She stepped forward and tugged at the white beard, pulling it away from his face.

Her eyes got big. Her mouth opened so wide, her jaw almost hit the floor.

"You're that cop," she blurted. "The one who wrote me that ticket."

Santa smiled sheepishly. He looked down at the floor.

"This is my wife, Jill," he said introducing the elf. The young woman grinned.

"I hated you," Michelle said.

"I know," he said laughing. He put his beard back in place. "The kids think I'm real."

"But how did you find me?"

"I already had your address. I asked around, did some checking, talked to lotsa folks. You know, cop stuff. Do you really think I look like a Martian?"

Michelle's face flushed; her lips tightened. She had told the traffic ticket story to just about everyone and always at the police officer's expense.

"I couldn't fix the ticket," he said. "So Jill and I ... we decided the next best thing was to fix your Christmas."

"Merry Christmas," Jill said. She reached out and hugged Michelle.

"Mom, Mom," called Jared. "Come and see how this works!" Brandon clapped his little hands.

"That must have cost you a fortune," Michelle said. "I know those games are scarce, and they are not cheap."

"We found the game for sale on eBay," Jill said.

"Oh." Michelle's dark eyes were tearing; her voice choked. "I don't know how to thank you."

"Mommy! Mommy!" Brandon called.

"You have a nice day, ma'am," Santa said in his police-officer voice. Then they were gone.

Michelle stood for a moment looking at the closed door, until she realized she was still holding the small package. She pulled away the bow and opened it. Inside was a gift card for Safeway and a note with a telephone number scrawled at the top:

Please call me after the holidays. In my real life, I am a social worker. I can help you get the services you need—Jill (the elf.)

"I didn't even get his name," Michelle said aloud.

"Whose name?" asked Jared who suddenly stood in front of her. "I'm going to call Dad and tell him Santa came and brought the Rambo Danbo, just like he said."

"You better wait, Jared." Michelle felt a pang of anger that Jerry was somehow the hero of this magical moment. She would have loved to jolt Jerry out of bed, but she feared a woman might answer, and Jared would not understand.

"Your dad is probably still asleep. Let's eat breakfast. You can call him later."

She put slices of bread in the toaster and poured the milk

over their Cheerios. Jared brought the Rambo Danbo to the table, and Brandon twirled the propeller of his blue airplane. Soon little boy chatter and the smell of toast and peanut butter filled their apartment.

Michelle poured herself a second cup of coffee and pulled open the blind over the kitchen sink. Outside the weather was changing. Bright sunlight, winning its struggle over the gray overcast sky, streamed through the glass, making the ornaments on the little philodendron sparkle.

ACKNOWLEDGMENTS

Special thanks to Lois Rosen, Jane Fernandez, and Dawn Eisler Smith.

ABOUT THE AUTHOR

Jean Rover lives and writes in Oregon's lush Willamette Valley where she cares for thirty rose bushes, her dog, Shanti, and cat, Mr. B.C. Kitty, both rescued animals. Her writing has appeared in *Gold Man Review*, *Work Literary Magazine*, *Rose Red Review*, *Paper Tape Literary Magazine*, the *This I Believe* project and various periodicals. She earned degrees in English and Journalism from the University of Oregon, holds an MBA from Willamette University, and has an extensive background in corporate and marketing communications. She is an award-winning business communicator. Her novels *Touch The Sky* and its sequel, *Ready or Not,* are looking for publishers.

www.ingramcontent.com/pod-product-compliance
Lightning Source LLC
Chambersburg PA
CBHW071209130626
46555CB00004B/1642